The Little Kids' Table

Written by
Mary Ann McCabe Riehle

and

Illustrated by
Mary Reaves Uhles

I love when we visit my grandma Mabel.
I get to sit at the little kids' table!

The grown-ups' table is so shiny and fancy,
and has pretty flowers from my aunt Nancy.

When my grandma calls out,

"Let's eat!"

Like in musical chairs, we race for our seats.

We run super fast—
we're almost flying!
But my brother gets bumped
and ends up crying.

Next to our forks we have spoons at our places.
We try to get them to stick to our faces.

First you breathe on the spoon, then press it on tight.
It'll hang from your nose if you do it just right.

Mom piles food high on all of our plates,
making us try the foods we know we'll hate.
I have no idea why it's my mom's goal
to have us all love broccoli casserole.

'Cause even if you are not very picky there are some foods that are totally icky.

Grandma says, "You might like it. You never know!
If you don't eat your veggies, how will you grow?"

We play tricks at this table—don't leave your seat.
You might come back to a meal you won't want to eat.

Peas in your milk or some messy ketchup grins—
two of the favorites from my cousins, the twins.

We get super silly—you know how that goes—
You start laughing so hard
milk squirts from your nose.

But before someone chokes on their mac 'n cheese,
Mom gives us the look that says

"Stop it now, please!"

But in comes crashing
my grandpa's dog Daisy.

With her jumping and barking
it gets even more crazy!

He says she's part lab, another part poodle,
and calls her his sweet little Labradoodle.

Giggle, gulp, clatter, and **munch**.
Icky, sticky, crash, and **crunch!**

Our parents look over and tell us to hush,

but I think they wish they were still one of us.

Because I can see it in Uncle Fred's eye,
at the end of the meal when it's time for pie.

With a grin on his face he gives us a wink.
He'd rather sit here, at least that's what I think.

I bet if grown-ups were granted three wishes,
one would be to give up those fancy dishes.

And go back to the days when they were able to sit again at the little kids' table.

Because we all know when the meal is done,

To my daughters, Bridget and Ellen, and all of my nieces
and nephews. Your antics, fun, and laughter while seated at
the little kids' table have been an inspiration and a blessing.

Mary Ann McCabe Riehle

For the family around my table especially Mother, Daddy,
Jackson, Grace and Mike, who traveled the farthest.

Mary Reaves Uhles

Sleeping Bear Press
2395 South Huron Parkway, Suite 200
Ann Arbor, MI 48104
www.sleepingbearpress.com

Printed and bound in the United States.

10 9 8 7 6 5 4 3 2 1

Library of Congress Cataloging-in-Publication Data

Riehle, Mary Ann McCabe, 1959-
The little kids' table / by Mary Ann McCabe Riehle ; illustrated by Mary Uhles.
pages cm
Summary: "Everyone knows that the little kids' table is the place to be for any
holiday or family gathering. This silly, rhyming story follows a group of rambunctious
cousins from table setting to dessert. A universal theme, The Little Kids' Table will
have kids—and parents!—howling with laughter"—Provided by the publisher.
ISBN 978-1-58536-913-3
1. Table etiquette—Juvenile poetry 2. Table etiquette—Juvenile humor.
3. Dinners and dining—Juvenile poetry. 4. Dinners and dining—Juvenile humor.
I. Uhles, Mary, 1972- illustrator. II. Title.
PS3618.I39245L68 2015
811'.6—dc23   2015001601